MIXED MARTIAL ARTS

MMA: FEMALE FIGHTERS

Frazer Andrew Krohn

Abdo & Daughters
MIDDLE GRADE NONFICTION

An imprint of Abdo Publishing
abdobooks.com

ABDOBOOKS.COM

Published by Abdo Publishing, a division of ABDO, PO Box 398166, Minneapolis, Minnesota 55439. Copyright © 2023 by Abdo Consulting Group, Inc. International copyrights reserved in all countries. No part of this book may be reproduced in any form without written permission from the publisher. Abdo & Daughters™ is a trademark and logo of Abdo Publishing.

102022
012023

THIS BOOK CONTAINS RECYCLED MATERIALS

Design: Kelly Doudna, Mighty Media, Inc.
Production: Mighty Media, Inc.
Editor: Liz Salzmann
Cover Photograph: John Locher/AP Images
Interior Photographs: A.RICARDO/Shutterstock Images, pp. 8-9, 11, 21, 27, 30, 44, 54–55, 60 (top right); Andre Luiz Moreira/Shutterstock Images, p. 18; Andy Brownbill/AP Images, p. 32 (top); Brandon Wade/AP Images, p. 36; Carlos Montoya/Shutterstock Images, p. 31; Cassiano Correia/Shutterstock Images, p. 59 (bottom); Charles Dharapak/AP Images, p. 26; Chase Stevens/AP Images, pp. 45, 61 (bottom right); Damian Dovarganes/AP Images, p. 28 (bottom); Dawid S Swierczek/Shutterstock Images, p. 41; Denis Makarenko/Shutterstock Images, p. 16; Etsuo Hara/Getty Images, p. 58; Everyonephoto Studio/Shutterstock Images, pp. 10, 60 (top left); Featureflash Photo Agency/Shutterstock Images, p. 37; G Holland/Shutterstock Images, p. 39; Gregory Payan/AP Images, p. 7; Icon Sports Wire/Getty Images, p. 20; Jae C. Hong/AP Images, p. 28 (top); Jason Franson/AP Images, p. 13 (top); Jayne Kamin-Oncea/Getty Images, p. 50; Jeff Chiu/AP Images, pp. 12, 61 (bottom left); John Locher/AP Images, pp. 17 (bottom), 33, 43; Kathy Hutchins/Shutterstock Images, pp. 24–25; Kobby Dagan/Shutterstock Images, pp. 48–49; Kyusung Gong/AP Images, p. 47; Louis Grasse/PxImages/AP Images, pp. 22, 38 (bottom), 56; Mark J. Terrill/AP Images, p. 29; Michael Dunn/Wikimedia Commons, pp. 13 (right), 60 (bottom); Mwsportsart/Shutterstock Images, pp. 40, 57; Nox Yang/Image Press Agency/AP Images, pp. 53 (top), 61 (top left); Photocarioca/Shutterstock Images, p. 53 (bottom); Salty View/Shutterstock Images, p. 51; Stephen McCarthy/Web Summit via Sportsfile/Wikimedia Commons, p. 17 (top); Steve Marcus/AP Images, pp. 4–5, 6, 38 (top), 61 (top right); Tinseltown/Shutterstock Images, p. 32 (bottom); Tofudevil/Shutterstock Images, p. 52; Wikimedia Commons, pp. 14–15, 19, 34–35, 46, 59 (top)
Design Elements: Mighty Media, Inc.; mkirarslan/iStockphoto; sanchesnet1/iStockphoto

Library of Congress Control Number: 2022940768

Publisher's Cataloging-in-Publication Data

Names: Krohn, Frazer Andrew, author.
Title: MMA: female fighters / by Frazer Andrew Krohn
Description: Minneapolis, Minnesota : Abdo Publishing, 2023 | Series: Mixed martial arts | Includes online resources and index.
Identifiers: ISBN 9781532199202 (lib. bdg.) | ISBN 9781098274405 (ebook)
Subjects: LCSH: MMA (Mixed martial arts)--Juvenile literature. | Mixed martial arts--Juvenile literature. | Hand-to-hand fighting--Juvenile literature. | Female athletes--Juvenile literature. | Women martial artists--Juvenile literature. | Ultimate fighting--Juvenile literature. | Sports--History--Juvenile literature.
Classification: DDC 796.81--dc23

CONTENTS

The Greatest Women's Fight of All Time 5
Women in Mixed Martial Arts 9
Pioneers in Women's MMA 15
Ronda Rousey 25
Women in the UFC 35
Women outside the UFC 49
Looking to the Future 55
Timeline 60

Glossary 62
Online Resources 63
Index 64

Zhang (*right*) aims a powerful punch at Jędrzejczyk's face during their epic battle.

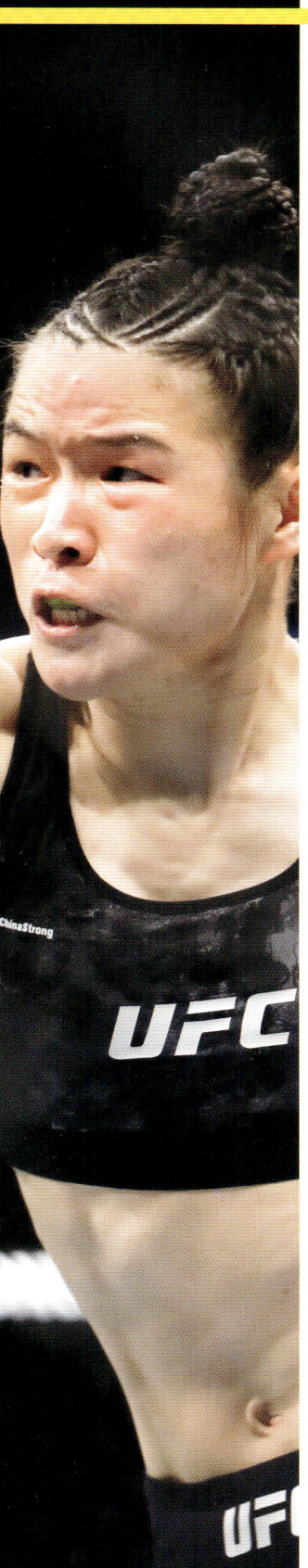

CHAPTER 1

THE GREATEST WOMEN'S FIGHT OF ALL TIME

It was March 7, 2020. T-Mobile Arena in Las Vegas, Nevada, was packed for the Ultimate Fighting Championship (UFC) event UFC 248. One of the two headline fights was the strawweight championship bout between two female mixed martial arts (MMA) powerhouses.

Polish fighter Joanna Jędrzejczyk was a former champion. She won the title at UFC 185 in March 2015. Jędrzejczyk then went undefeated for the next two years before losing the championship in November 2017. Now, Jędrzejczyk faced the current champion, Zhang Weili of China. Zhang had won her last 20 fights.

The back-and-forth fight saw both women leave it all in the Octagon. They stood toe to toe, each willing to take a number of shots in order to

The 2020 UFC 248 fight between Zhang (*left*) and Jędrzejczyk (*right*) was an exciting, action-packed event.

land her own. Throwing a combined 783 strikes, both fighters were determined to walk away with the championship belt.

Both women were bloodied and bruised. Jędrzejczyk's forehead was so swollen she was nearly unrecognizable. But by the final bell, neither woman had won the fight. So, the winner was decided by the judges. Zhang won in a split decision, meaning two of the three judges named her the winner. The third judge said Jędrzejczyk won.

The Jędrzejczyk–Zhang fight received Fight of the Night honors at the event. It was also named 2020 Fight of the Year by several publications. And in March 2022, sports media company *Sporting News* ranked it the number one women's MMA fight of all time. It will take something truly extraordinary to beat it.

Zhang beat Jéssica Andrade (*pictured*) on August 31, 2019, to win the strawweight title.

Though women were not permitted to fight in the UFC for nearly 20 years, many women, including Amanda Nunes (*left*) and Raquel Pennington (*right*), compete in the promotion today.

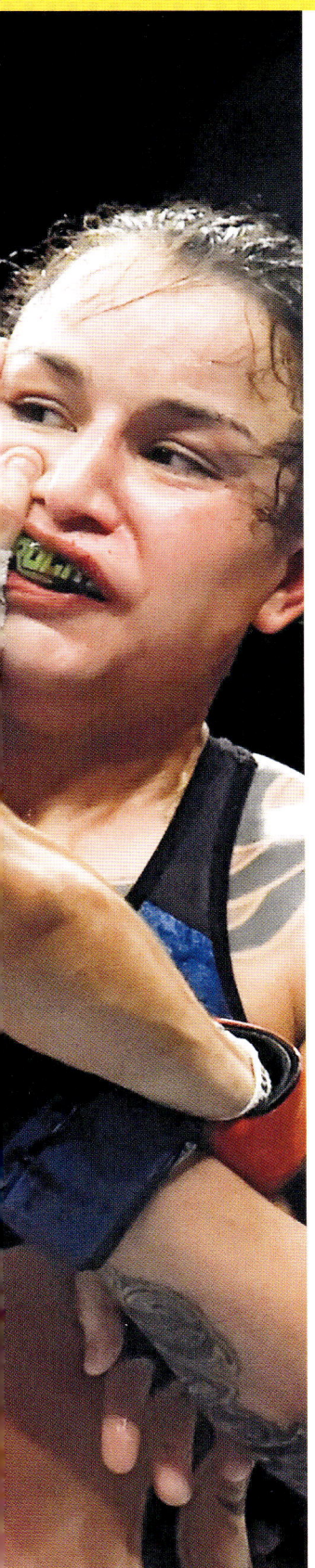

CHAPTER 2

WOMEN IN MIXED MARTIAL ARTS

Combat sports have long been dominated by men. Historically, women weren't allowed to compete at the highest levels. They were often restricted to regional competitions. Over time, this has changed and today there are many MMA events featuring female fighters.

THE HISTORY OF WOMEN IN MMA

MMA has historical roots, with hand-to-hand combat dating back to ancient Greece. Fast forward to Brazil in the 1920s and we get the introduction of Vale Tudo. The name *Vale Tudo* is Portuguese for "everything allowed." Vale Tudo included Brazilian jiu-jitsu (BJJ), which is still a popular form of martial arts today. Then in 1993, BJJ fighter Rorion Gracie and businessman Art Davie established the UFC. Its first event, UFC 1, signaled the arrival of MMA in the mainstream.

Although the UFC didn't include women until 2013, there were female MMA fighters earlier than that. The International Fighting Championships (IFC) was established in 1996. On March 28, 1997, the IFC held the first sanctioned women's MMA fight in the United States. The fight was held at the Akwesasne Mohawk Casino in Hogansburg, New York. Becky Levi defeated Betty Fagan in less than two minutes with a technical knockout (TKO).

The Levi–Fagan fight sparked interest in women's MMA. Soon, promotions such as Strikeforce, EliteXC, and Bellator were all regularly putting on women's fights. Strikeforce, in particular, took an interest in the women's MMA game. It signed a number of highly regarded female prospects in order to help build its brand.

The first all-female promotion, Smackgirl, was founded in Japan in 2001. It did a lot to aid the growth of female MMA. Smackgirl officially disbanded in 2008 and was rebranded into Jewels that same year. Jewels didn't make huge waves itself, but it inspired another all-female promotion, Invicta Fighting Championships. Invicta FC was established in 2012 and is the prominent all-female promotion. Many of its fighters go on to join bigger promotions, such as the UFC and Bellator.

Brazilian jiu-jitsu is an important aspect of today's MMA.

There are hundreds of UFC fights every year.

ULTIMATE FIGHTING CHAMPIONSHIP

The Ultimate Fighting Championship is, without a doubt, the premier MMA promotion in the world. Founded in 1993, the UFC would become the first mainstream MMA promotion. Those in the UFC had to deal with the setbacks, aid in rule progression, and be accountable for any early missteps. As the popularity of MMA grew, the UFC created more weight classes in order to make fights safer, fairer, and more competitive. Today, it's widely accepted that UFC champions are the best MMA fighters in the world.

Marloes Coenen (*left*) and Sarah Kaufman (*right*) fight in a Strikeforce event in 2010.

A KEY NIGHT IN WOMEN'S MMA

A pivotal night in women's MMA history occurred on August 15, 2009. That night *Strikeforce: Carano vs. Cyborg* aired on the television network Showtime. This event marked the first time two women headlined a major MMA event. The winner would be crowned the first Strikeforce women's featherweight champion. This event was a huge step forward for women's MMA, as they were finally given the stage to demonstrate their talents.

The main fight featured American Gina Carano against Cris Cyborg of Brazil. Carano was the undefeated favorite of women's MMA. Cyborg was a rising star with multiple knockouts and an exciting fighting style. After 4 minutes and 59 seconds, Cyborg finished Carano with brutal strikes to win the title.

UFC fighters Felicia Spencer (*left*) and Cyborg (*right*) are both former Invicta FC fighters.

This proved to be Carano's last fight. She retired from MMA and began an acting career. Cyborg continued her rise in MMA. She defended her Strikeforce title multiple times. She also won the first Invicta FC featherweight belt, won the UFC women's featherweight belt, and became the Bellator featherweight champion.

About 576,000 people watched the Strikeforce fight between Carano (*left*) and Cyborg (*right*) on Showtime.

Since retiring from competition, Gracie (*top*) focuses on teaching jiu-jitsu.

CHAPTER 3

PIONEERS IN WOMEN'S MMA

Royce Gracie is without a doubt the most well-known pioneer in men's MMA. The winner of UFC 1, UFC 2, and UFC 4, Gracie showed the world just how effective his martial art, BJJ, was. Gracie set the precedent for many future stars and showed what it takes to become an elite mixed martial artist.

Although budding female MMA fighters can look up to male stars, who were the pioneers in women's MMA? Who broke the mold and pushed for women to become more prominent in the male-dominated sport? Let's take a look at some of the fighters who aided the growth of the sport for women.

GINA CARANO

Gina Carano

Carano's 2009 fight against Cyborg was an important moment in women's MMA. But it was largely possible because Carano was already a big star. She was known as "the face of women's MMA." Carano started training in Muay Thai in the early 2000s and achieved a 12-1 record in Muay Thai competitions.

In 2006, Carano transitioned to MMA. She joined Strikeforce, becoming the promotion's first female fighter. Her fame and success led to Strikeforce making her 2009 bout with Cyborg the first women's fight to headline a major MMA event. Without Carano, women's MMA would not have taken off as quickly as it did. She went on to have a successful career in acting. One of her most famous roles was as Cara Dune in the TV series *The Mandalorian*.

CRIS CYBORG

Similar to Carano, a discussion of pioneers in women's MMA would not be complete without including fighter Cris Cyborg. Following her victory over Carano in that historic 2009 fight, her career rose quickly. Cyborg had lost her first MMA fight in 2005. Then she won every fight for the next 13 years. Cyborg dominated opponents with her size, punching power, and impressive ground game.

Cyborg started out with Strikeforce before moving to Invicta FC. The UFC recognized her star power and in 2015 signed her to its women's featherweight division. Cyborg defeated Tonya Evinger to win her first UFC featherweight title in 2017. Cyborg lost her featherweight belt to

Cris Cyborg

The UFC created a featherweight division so that Cyborg would join the promotion.

Amanda Nunes the next year, but Cyborg bounced back and won her next fight, which was her last with the UFC.

In 2019, Cyborg signed with Bellator. She has dominated every opponent thus far. She's seen as one of the heaviest hitters in the history of women's MMA, with 20 of her 26 wins coming by knockout.

MIESHA TATE

Miesha Tate's nickname Cupcake hardly describes her fierce fighting style, but she is a true savage in MMA. One of the true pioneers of the sport, Tate has been competing since 2006. Originally a wrestler, Tate transitioned into MMA that year. She had three amateur fights before turning professional in 2007. After making a name for herself in small regional events, Tate debuted with Strikeforce in 2008. She soon became a star on the women's Strikeforce roster,

Miesha Tate

winning the Strikeforce women's bantamweight title in 2011.

The next year, a rivalry between Tate and Ronda Rousey developed. Rousey was set to be Tate's first challenger for her Strikeforce bantamweight belt, and the two clearly had bad blood. Their personalities clashed, and their comments about each other helped their fight gain attention. Their March 3, 2012, title bout marked the first time that two women headlined a major event since Cyborg vs. Carano in 2009. Rousey defeated Tate in the first round to win the Strikeforce bantamweight title.

Tate with her bantamweight championship belt in 2016

Tate joined the UFC in 2013 and challenged Rousey for the UFC bantamweight title. But again she lost. It wasn't until UFC 196 in March 2016 that Tate finally realized her goal of becoming a UFC champion. She defeated the current champion Holly Holm to secure the UFC women's bantamweight title. Although she retired in 2016, she returned to action in 2021 to try to regain the UFC bantamweight title.

Fujii (*left*) in a 2010 fight against Carla Esparza

MEGUMI FUJII

Japanese fighter Megumi Fujii isn't the most well-known name in women's MMA, but she was no doubt a pioneer of the sport. In particular, she did a lot to bring Asian women's MMA to the mainstream. With a history in judo and BJJ, Fujii transitioned into MMA in 2004, joining Smackgirl. After making a name for herself in Japan, Fujii had a 19-0 record before signing with Bellator. She entered into the strawweight tournament, picking up two victories

Rousey with her UFC bantamweight belt

ROUSEY VS. CYBORG?

Ronda Rousey rose to stardom by taking on all challengers. Except one. Fans would have loved to see her fight Cris Cyborg. But Rousey would only face Cyborg in a bantamweight fight. Rousey sometimes fought bigger opponents, but Cyborg had tested positive for anabolic steroids, so Rousey was extra cautious. She felt it would only be fair if the fight was at her weight. But Cyborg was unable to get down to the bantamweight limit of 135 pounds (61.2 kg). So, the fight didn't happen. Many think Cyborg would beat Rousey on foot, with Rousey dominating on the ground. But we'll never know how it would have gone.

before losing in the final. Fujii continued fighting until she retired in 2013 with a career 26-3 record.

ROXANNE MODAFFERI

Roxanne Modafferi had a long, storied career in MMA. She debuted in 2003 and retired in 2022. Over her career, she fought everywhere. From Smackgirl to Ring of Combat, Strikeforce to Cage Warriors, and Invicta FC to the UFC, Modafferi was a recognizable face throughout women's MMA.

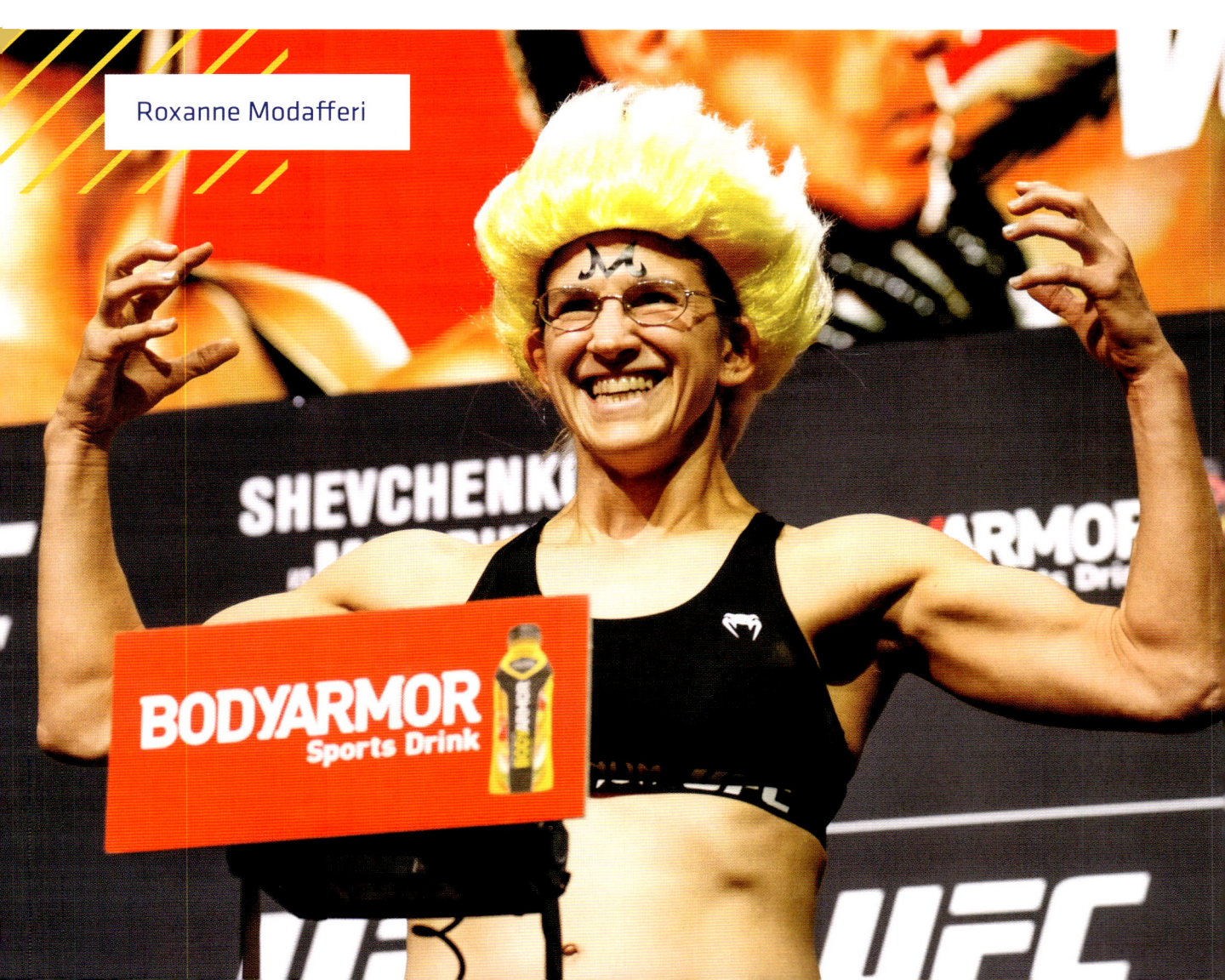

Roxanne Modafferi

Highlights of Modafferi's career include winning titles with Fatal Femmes Fighting, Fusion Fight League, and Invicta FC. She also fought title bouts with Strikeforce and the UFC but never won with those promotions. But she was always in the game, with most of her fights ending in judges' decisions.

Modafferi also pulled off a major upset in 2020. She dominated the undefeated Maycee Barber, handing the up-and-coming Barber her first loss. Modafferi retired in 2022 with the most women's MMA fights in history, cementing her standing as a true pioneer.

FIGHTIN' WORDS

Here are some common terms used in MMA.

FIGHT CARD // a program or list of the matches during an MMA event. The card usually has one or two headline, or main, matches plus several warm-up, or preliminary, matches.

GRAPPLE // to fight using throws, takedowns, holds, and other wrestling moves rather than punches or kicks.

KNOCKOUT (KO) // when one fighter has been knocked down and is unable to get up and resume fighting within a specified time.

ROUND // one of the periods of time a fight is divided into. MMA fights have three or five five-minute rounds with a one-minute rest between each round.

STRIKE // a blow delivered to an opponent while standing. A strike can be made by a fist, knee, elbow, or foot.

SUBMISSION // when a fighter wins by grabbing their opponent in a painful hold that they can't break free of, so that they are forced to give up.

TAKEDOWN // a move that forces or knocks an opponent to the ground.

TAP OUT // when a fighter taps the mat with their hand to indicate that they want to give up.

TECHNICAL KNOCKOUT (TKO) // when a fight referee stops a match because one of the fighters is too injured to continue.

Rousey (left) with White

CHAPTER 4

RONDA ROUSEY

A discussion of pioneers in women's MMA wouldn't be complete without Ronda Rousey. She became one of the most recognizable faces in the history of the UFC and one of its biggest pay-per-view (PPV) stars ever. The UFC started signing female fighters later than many other promotions. In 2011, UFC president Dana White was recorded saying, "Never!" when asked when the UFC would have women's fights. But he changed his tune when Rousey's domination in Strikeforce showed that she could be a superstar.

FROM JUDO TO MMA

At age 11, Rousey started training in judo with her mother, who had become the first American to win a World Judo Championship in 1984. From the beginning, Rousey had a relentless work ethic. She won the World Championship silver medal in 2007 and then represented the United States in the 2008 Olympic Games. She came home with a bronze medal in the 70 kg division. This marked the first time an American won an Olympic medal in women's judo.

By 2010, Rousey transitioned to MMA, starting with wins in three amateur bouts. None of them lasted more than one minute. Rousey made her professional debut in 2011 with Strikeforce, winning her first four fights. Then she faced Tate in the bantamweight title fight on March 3, 2012. Rousey defeated Tate in the first round, becoming the Strikeforce bantamweight champion. In August that year she defended her title with a defeat of Sarah Kaufman. Rousey was sitting at 6-0, with all wins coming in the first round and all by armbar submission.

Rousey (*right*) defeated Annett Böhm of Germany to win a bronze medal at the 2008 Olympics.

SIGNING WITH THE UFC

In November 2012, Rousey made history by becoming the first woman to sign with the UFC. Dana White made her an exception to his "no women" rule. He described Rousey as having "the whole package." He was not wrong. Rousey had a dynamic, appealing personality as well as an exciting, brutal, and devastating fighting style. With six straight dominating wins, it was impossible for Rousey not to get noticed in the mainstream.

Rousey's UFC debut was set for February 2013 at UFC 157. This was a huge step forward for women's MMA. Not only were women finally getting the spotlight they deserved, but Rousey's fight was the headliner. She faced another MMA pioneer, Liz Carmouche. Carmouche had an 8-2 record and had competed for the Strikeforce bantamweight title before Rousey held it.

Prior to the bout, Rousey was a huge favorite. She was the defending champion, had defeated all of her opponents, and had never needed more than one round to win. But Carmouche nearly had Rousey early on in the fight. Following a grappling exchange, Carmouche ended up on Rousey's back, squeezing her jaw and chin. The force that Carmouche applied to Rousey's face visibly affected

Rousey's personality and fighting style have won her many fans.

the champion. But Rousey was able to get free of Carmouche's hold. She quickly secured an armbar to defeat Carmouche and retain her title.

Later that year, Rousey was selected to be a coach on the MMA reality TV show *The Ultimate Fighter*. The other coach

Rousey (*top*) competed against Carmouche (*bottom*) in the first-ever UFC women's fight.

Rousey (*left*) and Carmouche at the weigh-in before their fight

was her rival Miesha Tate. During the show, they faced each other in a rematch. This fight marked the first time that Rousey was unable to finish a fight in the first round. But in the third round, Rousey secured yet another armbar submission, winning the fight. The Rousey-Tate bout was named Fight of the Night.

From 2013 to 2015, Rousey defended her UFC bantamweight title six times. This included beating Sara McMann, Alexis Davis, and Cat Zingano. Davis and Zingano were both finished in under

Rousey (*right*) set a record for quickest finish in UFC history when Zingano (*left*) tapped out in 14 seconds.

Rousey (*left*) responded to Correia's (*right*) taunts with a brutal finish.

20 seconds. The finish of Zingano in just 14 seconds set the record for the quickest finish in UFC championship fight history. This record stood until 2015, when Conor McGregor knocked out José Aldo in 13 seconds.

Rousey's final title defense came against Brazilian fighter Bethe Correia. The two had a bitter confrontation before the fight, where Correia made personal comments about Rousey's family. Rousey responded with her fists, knocking out Correia in just 36 seconds. This extended Rousey's undefeated run to 12-0. She was at the top of her fighting game, as well as a major PPV star. Then it all came crashing down.

LOSSES AND RETIREMENT

On November 14, 2015, Rousey faced the undefeated former world champion boxer, Holly Holm. Again, Rousey entered the bout a heavy favorite. However, Holm dominated Rousey throughout the fight. She made Rousey miss her shots in an embarrassing manner, easily slipping underneath wild swings from Rousey.

At the start of the second round, it was clear that Rousey needed to close the distance between herself and Holm and try to use her judo background to get Holm to the ground. Unfortunately for the champion, this would be her downfall. She tried to grab hold of Holm, who shook her off and landed one of the most brutal head kicks in MMA history. It knocked Rousey out cold. She lost the title to Holm.

Holly Holm

The fight was named Fight of the Night, and Holm won Knockout of the Year for 2015 as well. Holms's win was one of the biggest upsets in UFC history, since Rousey had been so dominant before the fight. Although Holm was a solid fighter, many believed that Rousey was unbeatable. But her flaws were clear. In particular, her stand-up game was poor at the highest level.

This glaring weakness would become even more evident in her next fight. After more than a year away from competition, Rousey returned to challenge the current bantamweight champion, Amanda Nunes. Unfortunately, Nunes was too powerful and was a superior striker. Rousey's defense wasn't able to withstand Nunes's

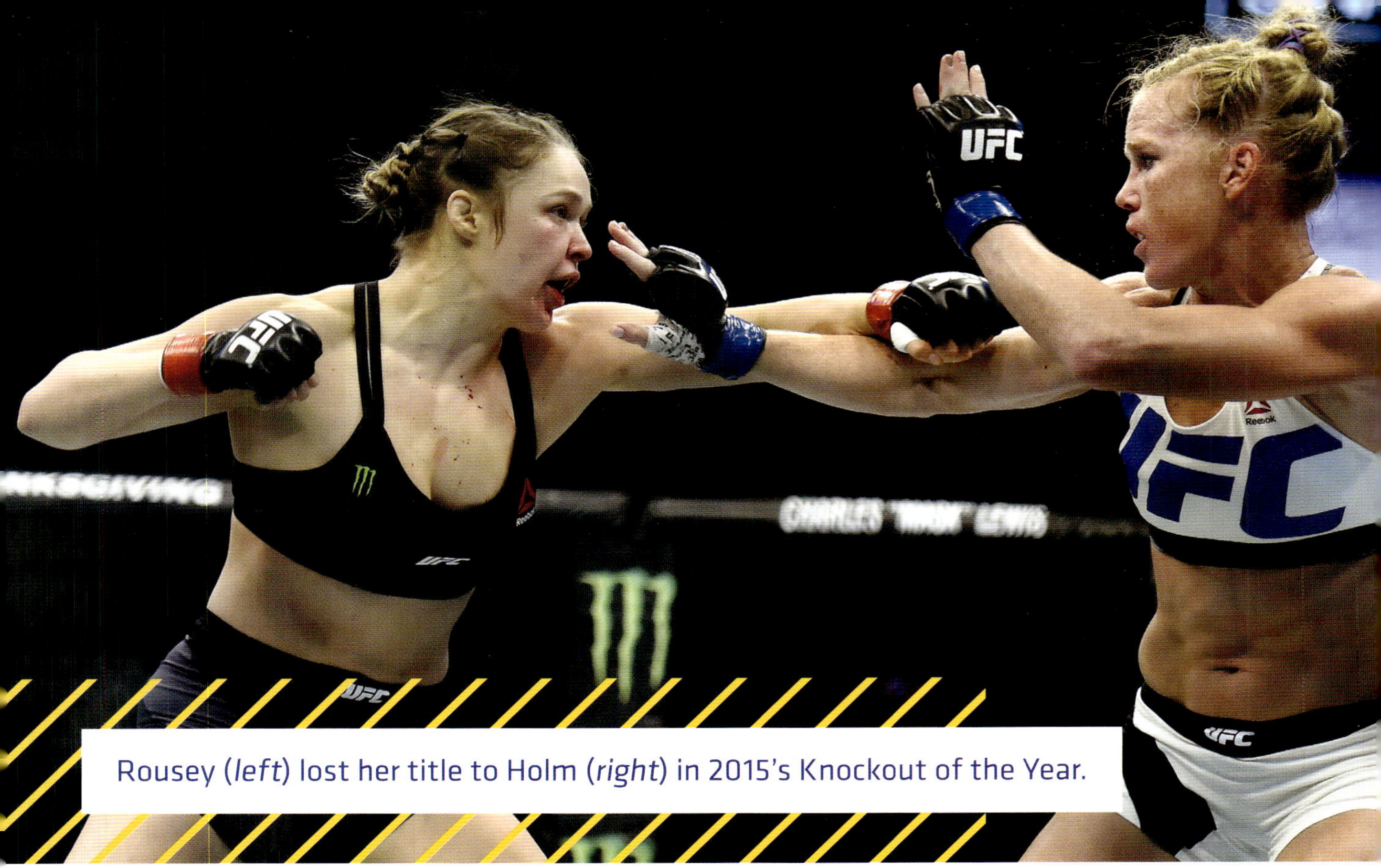

Rousey (*left*) lost her title to Holm (*right*) in 2015's Knockout of the Year.

Rousey has focused on WWE and acting over the past few years.

strong punches. Rousey's return wasn't triumphant and lasted just 48 seconds.

After Rousey lost to Nunes, she switched to wrestling and has become a World Wrestling Entertainment (WWE) champion. Rousey has also appeared in multiple films and TV shows. Her film career began when she was still UFC champion, which some people have suggested is why her MMA career went downhill. They believe she was focusing too much on acting and not enough on fighting. While she hasn't officially declared herself retired from MMA, Rousey has said it's very unlikely she'll fight again. But she will always be remembered for her dominance during the height of her career and for her contributions to advancing women in MMA.

Rousey (*right*) suffered another major defeat against Nunes (*left*) in 2016.

Carla Esparza became the UFC's first strawweight champion in 2014.

CHAPTER 5

WOMEN IN THE UFC

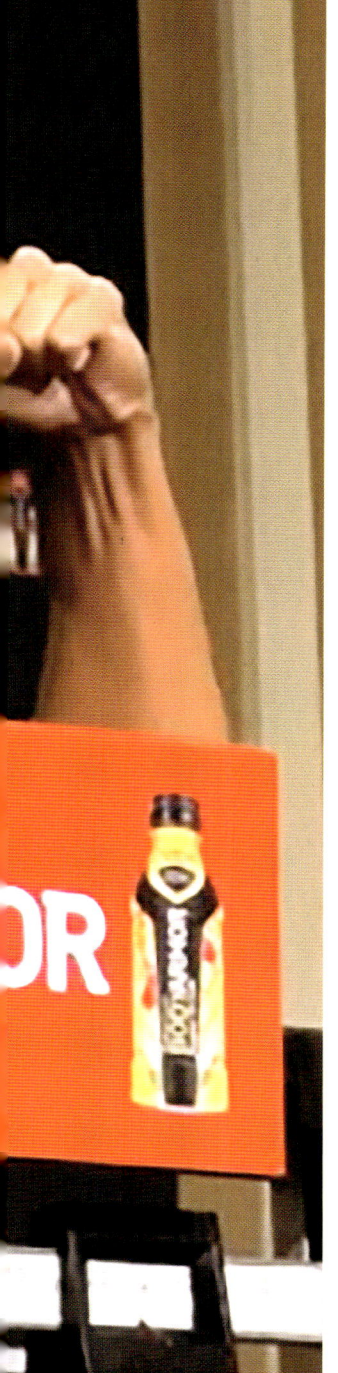

Rousey was the first woman to compete in the UFC, the first female champion, and the first major female star in the sport, but she's not the only female UFC fighter to become a star. The four women's divisions provide four title belts to compete for, so there are four reigning champions.

The divisions are based on a fighter's weight. They are strawweight (106 to 115 pounds), flyweight (116 to 125 pounds), bantamweight (126 to 135 pounds), and featherweight (136 to 145 pounds). The featherweight division often has very few fighters, so the title is rarely fought over. As of 2022, Amanda Nunes was the champion, but there were few other featherweights on the UFC roster.

UFC STRAWWEIGHT DIVISION

The UFC strawweight division was introduced in 2014 during the twentieth season of *The Ultimate Fighter*. The final fight was between Carla Esparza and Rose Namajunas. Esparza finished Namajunas in the third round to become the first strawweight champion.

Esparza would only hold the title for three months before she faced undefeated Polish fighter Joanna Jędrzejczyk. With a background in Muay Thai and kickboxing, Jędrzejczyk had an 8-0 record before challenging Esparza. As the fight played out, it was clear that the Polish star was far superior to Esparza. The champion

Jędrzejczyk (*left*) beat Esparza (*right*) for the strawweight title at UFC 185 in Dallas, Texas.

had trouble landing strikes as Jędrzejczyk dominated her way to a technical knockout finish.

Jędrzejczyk quickly became one of the UFC's most dominant fighters. She successfully defended her title five times. Jędrzejczyk was also a coach on *The Ultimate Fighter*. She made appearances as the co-headliner at UFC 193 and UFC 205. In November 2017, Jędrzejczyk faced Rose Namajunas to defend her title a sixth time. The champion was a heavy favorite heading into the bout. However, Namajunas didn't care about the odds. Just three minutes into the bout, Jędrzejczyk's reign over the strawweight division came to an end. A strong combination sent Jędrzejczyk to the ground, where Namajunas jumped on her to finish the fight.

Over the next years, the belt continued to change hands. Namajunas lost it to Brazilian fighter Jéssica Andrade. In August 2019, Andrade got blown away by Zhang. Zhang made history by becoming the first Chinese-born champion, bringing many new Asian fans to the sport.

Namajunas won the strawweight championship in 2017.

37

In March 2020, Zhang put on one of the best UFC fights ever seen against Jędrzejczyk, coming out on top and retaining her belt.

However, Zhang then lost the title to Namajunas in April 2021. With this win,

Zhang was the first Chinese-born champion in UFC history.

In May 2022, Esparza (*bottom*) defeated Namajunas (*top*) to regain the UFC strawweight belt.

Paige VanZant

A QUICK RISE AND FALL

Making her UFC debut in 2014, Paige VanZant won four of her first five UFC fights, becoming an instant star. However, she then suffered a number of losses and injuries. In spite of this, she was still a star who drew fans. She had competed on the celebrity talent show *Dancing with the Stars* and had a large presence on social media. Due to her star power, the UFC had hoped to keep her on, but she simply wasn't good enough in the Octagon. After leaving the UFC, VanZant signed with Bare Knuckle Fighting Championship and All Elite Wrestling.

Namajunas became the first woman to regain a UFC belt after losing it. Later that year, the two had a rematch, with Namajunas successfully defending the title.

In 2022, Namajunas lost the strawweight belt in a rematch with Esparza. This is considered one of the least entertaining title fights in UFC history. There were only a combined 68 strikes in the 25-minute fight, leading to widespread criticism of both fighters' unexciting approach to the bout.

UFC FLYWEIGHT DIVISION

The newest division in the UFC, the flyweight division, was introduced in December 2017. It filled the 20-pound gap between the strawweight and bantamweight divisions. The flyweight division provides opportunities for a number of fighters who didn't easily fit into the earlier two. Like the strawweight division, the inaugural flyweight champion was determined by the outcome of a season of *The Ultimate Fighter*.

It was the twenty-sixth season of *The Ultimate Fighter*, and the final bout was between Nicco Montaño and Roxanne Modafferi, with

Shevchenko (*pictured*) defeated Jędrzejczyk for the flyweight title in 2018.

Montaño coming out the winner. However, Montaño was unable to defend her title because she couldn't maintain the required weight. So, the title was stripped from her. In December 2018, former bantamweight fighter Valentina Shevchenko faced former

Shevchenko (right) defends her title against Jessica Eye. She has successfully defended the title seven times.

strawweight champion Jędrzejczyk to fight for the flyweight title. Shevchenko won handily, becoming the second flyweight champion.

Since then, Shevchenko has reigned with an iron fist over the flyweight division, outclassing every opponent she has faced. What is most impressive about Shevchenko's title reign is that she beats her opponents at their own games. If she faces a wrestler, she'll outwrestle her; if she fights a Muay Thai fighter, she'll use her superior Muay Thai skills. She does the same against boxers and BJJ competitors. Shevchenko is 8-0 at flyweight, with an impressive four finishes. Her match with Jessica Eye is considered one of the greatest women's knockouts ever.

UFC BANTAMWEIGHT DIVISION

The UFC bantamweight division was the UFC's first women's division and is by far the most well-known division in all of women's MMA. It was established in December 2012, with Ronda Rousey as the inaugural champion. This marked the entrance of women to the UFC and MMA mainstream. Rousey defended her title six times before being defeated by Holly Holm in 2015.

Holm lost the title to Miesha Tate in her next match, and Tate lost to her first challenger, Amanda Nunes. With this win, Nunes became the first openly gay UFC champion, a pioneer in her own right. Nunes retained the title for over three years, successfully defending it five times. Two of these fights were against former champions Rousey and Holm.

Then Nunes faced Julianna Peña in December 2021. Peña won *The Ultimate Fighter* in 2013 but had to take time off in 2014 due

Nunes (*right*) defeated Tate (*left*) for the bantamweight championship at UFC 200 in Las Vegas.

to a bad injury. She then took more time off in 2017 to have a child. However, many believed she had the potential to be a star.

Nunes was expected to beat Peña as easily as she had her previous 12 opponents. Peña was the biggest underdog on the entire fight card. During the fight, Nunes dominated the first round,

Amanda Nunes in 2018

dropping Peña with multiple leg kicks and then dominating her on the ground. At the end of the round, the eventual outcome seemed obvious. But as the second round started, Peña began to land strikes with much more regularity, surprising the champion. Nunes was hurting, so she tried to end it quickly by diving in for a takedown. But Peña countered and jumped on Nunes's neck, forcing her to tap out.

Nunes (*left*) and Peña (*right*) were the coaches on season 30 of *The Ultimate Fighter*.

Peña's victory was arguably the biggest upset in UFC history. She didn't hold the title long, though. Nunes beat her in a rematch on July 30, 2022. That year, Peña and Nunes were chosen to be the coaches for the next season of *The Ultimate Fighter*.

UFC FEATHERWEIGHT DIVISION

The UFC women's featherweight division is the least active of the four women's divisions. It has no real fighters in the rankings and is basically dominated by one woman, Amanda Nunes. The division was created in February 2017, and the inaugural champion was Dutch fighter Germaine de Randamie. She was supposed to defend it against Cris Cyborg, but refused to fight her because of Cyborg's failed drug tests. Because of her refusal to fight, de Randamie was stripped of the title.

In July 2017, Cyborg defeated Tonya Evinger to win the vacant UFC featherweight title. She defended it twice and then faced Nunes. Nunes held the UFC bantamweight title. She wanted to beat Cyborg to become a two-weight champion. The fight that played out was an instant classic. The two women wasted no time in meeting in the middle and swinging away.

De Randamie (*pictured*) beat Holm to win the first UFC featherweight title.

Both women landed heavily on each other, with Nunes eventually getting the better of Cyborg, knocking her out to claim the belt. Nunes has defended the title twice, winning easily both times.

The featherweight title fight between Cyborg (*left*) and Nunes (*right*) was part of UFC 232.

ONE Championship is a martial arts promotion based in Asia.

CHAPTER 6

WOMEN OUTSIDE THE UFC

Although the women who compete in the UFC are seen as the best of the best, there are plenty of fighters outside of the UFC who could certainly compete with those in the "big leagues." Other promotions such as Invicta FC, the Professional Fighters League, and ONE Championship have some weight divisions that the UFC doesn't have. These include lightweight (146 to 155 pounds) and atomweight (96 to 105 pounds).

Some of the best martial artists in the world compete outside of the UFC. Cris Cyborg competed successfully in the UFC but signed with rival promotion, Bellator, in September 2019. She competed for the Bellator featherweight title in her first fight and hasn't taken a step backward since, dominating every opponent she's faced.

In addition, possibly the greatest women's fighter alive today competes for the Professional Fighters League and is yet to be truly tested. Kayla Harrison is a two-time Olympic gold medalist in judo, picking up medals in 2012 and 2016. In 2016, Harrison began to train in MMA, and made her debut in 2018. She competes in the lightweight division and has achieved two tournament victories. She's currently undefeated at 14–0 and has 11 finishes.

Harrison dominates every opponent she faces by using her judo skills to get the fight to the ground. It is possible that Harrison could be the best women's fighter today. However, because she doesn't

Cyborg is congratulated by Bellator president Scott Coker (*left*) after winning the Bellator featherweight belt.

Harrison (*second from left*) on the podium at the 2016 Olympics

compete against the best of the best, her true ability may never be known. Joining the UFC isn't currently an option for her because it doesn't have a women's lightweight division.

ONE Championship has a number of highly talented women in the lighter weight classes. Their atomweight champion, Angela Lee, has an 11–2 record and black belts in both BJJ and taekwondo. She became the youngest ever world champion in a major organization when she captured the ONE atomweight belt at 19 years old. A lifelong martial artist, Lee trains alongside her brother, Christian Lee, a former ONE lightweight champion.

Lee is a star fighter in the ONE Championship promotion.

Xiong Jing Nan competes for ONE Championship and holds the strawweight title. She was the first Chinese fighter to hold a belt in a major organization. She captured the belt in 2018 and is undefeated in the division, having successfully defended her title six times.

INVICTA FIGHTING CHAMPIONSHIPS

Invicta FC has arguably done more for female fighters than any other promotion. Created in 2012 by Shannon Knapp and Janet Martin, it is an all-women's promotion. With more than 50 events, Invicta FC has been developing female fighters since its creation. With five divisions, from atomweight (96 to 105 pounds) to featherweight (136 to 145 pounds), it provides plenty of opportunities for women throughout the weight classes. However, more often than not, the champion in any given division will soon vacate her belt to join a larger promotion, usually the UFC or Bellator. Women who have done this include Felicia Spencer, Cris Cyborg, Megan Anderson, and Jennifer Maia.

We can expect Invicta FC to continue to shape the women's MMA mold and put on competitive fights. There have been a number of former Invicta champions who have gone on to either hold or compete for UFC championships, and it's likely that in the future there will be many more women who leave Invicta FC to compete for UFC titles. It is seen as a feeder promotion, allowing women the chance to compete in competitive matchups within their own weight classes. The many women in the UFC and Bellator who have come from Invicta FC prove just how effective the promotion is at creating future stars.

Invicta FC president Shannon Knapp

Namajunas is one of many UFC stars to come from Invicta FC.

Rousey paved the way for women in the UFC.

CHAPTER 7

LOOKING TO THE FUTURE

In a relatively short time, women's MMA has gone from small shows with very few fans and almost no world-renowned stars to the mainstream. It is rare in today's MMA for a fight card to not include at least one women's fight.

Although Cyborg and Carano had brought women's MMA to the attention of many fans with their 2009 Strikeforce headlining event, they weren't the stars that the UFC was looking for. Prior to Ronda Rousey, the UFC didn't even consider signing women. Rousey broke the mold for female MMA fighters to make it into the big leagues. She was a huge success for the UFC, crossing over into the mainstream almost instantly and becoming a fighter that the company could build events around.

The post-Rousey era hasn't done nearly as well as when she was competing at the top of

Some fans have compared up-and-coming fighter Mackenzie Dern (*pictured*) to Rousey.

the sport. Women rarely headline events. Instead, a women's fight is more often the co-headliner or sometimes even the third fight on the card. Rousey headlined six PPV cards during her time in the UFC, allowing her to carry the mantle of not only women's MMA, but MMA as a whole. No female fighter since Rousey has transferred over to the mainstream as Rousey did.

SOCIAL MEDIA

In spite of the seemingly slow rise of women in MMA, the development of social media platforms has helped. Social media now plays much more of a factor in turning female fighters into megastars. When Rousey made her debut, Instagram was barely three years old. Since then, it has become vital in growing an athlete's brand. To become a huge UFC star today, a fighter not only has to perform inside the Octagon but also must have a large social media presence. This is certainly an aspect that is being improved and perfected by athletes in more recent years. It will be essential for another woman to make it to the top of the sport.

There is potential for female stars to rise to the top of the sport. The UFC is looking for a Rousey-type female megastar to carry the female side of the sport forward. But it has struggled to find her thus far.

ATOMWEIGHT DIVISION

Looking ahead, it appears vital that the UFC and Bellator add atomweight divisions

UFC fighters today, such as Andrea Lee, work to build a strong social media presence.

(96 to 105 pounds). As it stands, neither promotion offers this weight division, despite a large pool of talented fighters to sign. The next big star could be just around the corner but unable to progress because of limited weight classes.

A notable example is Michelle Waterson. Waterson won the Invicta FC atomweight title in 2013. She defended her title once before losing it. After this loss, Waterson moved up in weight to strawweight when she signed with the UFC. Although Waterson has won fights in that division, she's naturally a lighter weight fighter, which may be a reason why she hasn't quite made it to the championship level in the UFC. Waterson is undersized for the division, with other strawweights often being taller and physically stronger than she is. Waterson would benefit from being able to fight in an atomweight division.

The Invicta FC atomweight division is extremely deep and shows just how much talent there is in that weight class. A large number of

Kanna Asakura (*left*) and Ayaka Hamasaki (*right*) are top in the Rizin Fighting Federation's super atomweight class.

MMA ENDGAME

An MMA fight ends with either a finish or a judges' decision. A finish is when one fighter wins before the end of the rounds. This includes winning by submission, knockout, technical knockout, or disqualification. If neither fighter finishes by the end of the last round, then the winner is determined by the three fight judges. If all three judges choose the same winner, it's called a unanimous decision. If they don't all agree, it's called a split or majority decision. The winner is the fighter chosen by two of the judges.

atomweight fighters fight for Asian promotions, notably Rizin Fighting Federation. Opening up an atomweight division would allow the premier promotions to tap into the Asian market. Signing atomweight fighters from Asia would bring new eyes to the sport, new locations in which to host events, and other promotional opportunities.

With potential new weight divisions, developing megastars, and increased emphasis on including women in MMA, there is no doubt that the women's sport will continue to grow. High-level female MMA fighters will take advantage of these opportunities and put on a good show.

Michelle Waterson

Women such as Randa Markos (*left*) and Marina Rodriguez (*right*) continue to make their marks in the Octagon.

TIMELINE

Vale Tudo and Brazilian jiu-jitsu (BJJ) are developed.
1920s

The International Fighting Championships offers the first sanctioned women's MMA fight in the United States, featuring Becky Levi and Betty Fagan.
MARCH 28, 1997

Gina Carano becomes the first woman to join Strikeforce.
2006

1993
Rorion Gracie and Art Davie establish the Ultimate Fighting Championship and hold UFC 1.

2001
Smackgirl, the first all-female promotion, is founded in Japan.

The all-female promotion Invicta Fighting Championships is established.
2012

Zhang Weili defeats Joanna Jędrzejczyk at UFC 248.
MARCH 7, 2020

AUGUST 15, 2009
Strikeforce: Carano vs. Cyborg, the first major MMA event featuring a women's bout as a headliner, airs on Showtime.

NOVEMBER 2012
Ronda Rousey becomes the first woman to sign with the UFC.

DECEMBER 2021
Julianna Peña defeats Amanda Nunes in the biggest upset victory in UFC history.

GLOSSARY

anabolic steroid—a hormone used to help tissue grow that is sometimes abused by athletes to increase muscle size and strength despite possible harmful effects.

arguably—supported by reasons or evidence.

armbar—a common submission hold in which a competitor uses their body to apply pressure to their opponent's elbow to try to bend it backward.

brand—a public figure's style and reputation.

co-headliner—a fight at an MMA event that is nearly as important as the headliner.

debut—a first appearance.

disband—to break up something that is organized.

disqualification—barred from competition or from winning a prize or a contest.

hand-to-hand—a fight between two people that may involve weapons such as knives.

headliner—the most important fight at an MMA event. It is held last and is often a title fight.

inaugural—the first of a planned series of events.

mainstream—the ideas, attitudes, activities, or trends that are regarded as normal or dominant in society.

premier—first in rank, position, or importance.

promotion—an organization or company that organizes MMA fights and tournaments.

roster—a list of members.

sanctioned—approved by the state and monitored by the state athletic commission or other official organization. Sanctioned events follow defined procedures and standards to make sure that the fighters are safe.

vacate—to lose a title without losing a fight. Reasons a title can be vacated include long-term injury, switching weight classes or promotions, failing a drug test, and retiring from MMA.

work ethic—the determination to work hard to achieve a goal.

ONLINE RESOURCES

To learn more about female MMA fighters, please visit **abdobooklinks.com** or scan this QR code. These links are routinely monitored and updated to provide the most current information available.

INDEX

acting, 13, 16, 32–33
Akwesasne Mohawk Casino, 10
Aldo, José, 30
All Elite Wrestling, 39
Anderson, Megan, 53
Andrade, Jéssica, 37
Asia, 20, 37, 58

Barber, Maycee, 23
Bare Knuckle Fighting Championship, 39
Bellator, 10, 13, 18, 20, 49, 53, 57
boxing, 30, 42
Brazil, 9, 12, 30, 37
Brazilian jiu-jitsu (BJJ), 9, 15, 20, 42, 51

Cage Warriors, 22
Carano, Gina, 12–13, 16–17, 55
Carmouche, Liz, 27–28
China, 5, 37, 52
Correia, Bethe, 30
Cyborg, Cris, 12–13, 16–19, 21, 46, 49, 53, 55

Dancing with the Stars, 39
Davie, Art, 9
Davis, Alexis, 29–30
drugs, 21, 46

EliteXC, 10
Esparza, Carla, 36–37, 40
Evinger, Tonya, 17, 46
Eye, Jessica, 42

Fagan, Betty, 10
Fatal Femmes Fighting, 23
Fight of the Night, 7, 29, 31
Fight of the Year, 7
Fujii, Megumi, 20, 22
Fusion Fight League, 23

Gracie, Rorion, 9
Gracie, Royce, 15
Greece, 9

Harrison, Kayla, 50–51
Holm, Holly, 19, 30–31, 42

International Fighting Championships (IFC), 10
Invicta Fighting Championships, 10, 13, 17, 22–23, 49, 52–53, 57

Japan, 10, 20
Jędrzejczyk, Joanna, 5–7, 36–38, 42
Jewels, 10
judo, 20, 25–26, 31, 50

Kaufman, Sarah, 26
kickboxing, 36
Knapp, Shannon, 52
Knockout of the Year, 31

Lee, Angela, 51
Lee, Christian, 51
Levi, Becky, 10

Maia, Jennifer, 53
Mandalorian, The, 16
Martin, Janet, 52
McGregor, Conor, 30
McMann, Sara, 29
Modafferi, Roxanne, 22–23, 40–41
Montaño, Nicco, 40–41
Muay Thai, 16, 36, 42

Namajunas, Rose, 36–38, 40
Netherlands, The, 46
Nevada, 5
New York (state), 10
Nunes, Amanda, 18, 31–32, 35, 42–47

Octagon, 5, 39, 56
Olympic Games, 25–26, 50
ONE Championship, 49, 51–52

pay-per-view (PPV), 25, 30, 56
Peña, Juliana, 42–46
Poland, 5, 36–37
Portuguese, 9
Professional Fighters League, 49–50

Randamie, Germaine de, 46
Ring of Combat, 22
Rizin Fighting Federation, 58
Rousey, Ronda, 19, 21, 25–33, 35, 42, 55–56

Shevchenko, Valentina, 41–42
Showtime, 12
Smackgirl, 10, 20, 22
social media, 39, 56
Spencer, Felicia, 53
Sporting News, 7
Strikeforce, 10, 12–13, 16–19, 22–23, 25–27, 55

T-Mobile Arena, 5
taekwondo, 51
Tate, Miesha, 18–19, 26, 29, 42

Ultimate Fighter, The, 28, 36–37, 40–42, 46
Ultimate Fighting Championship (UFC), 5, 9–11, 13, 15, 17, 19, 22–23, 25, 27, 29–32, 35–40, 46, 49, 53, 55–57
United States, 10, 12, 25–26

Vale Tudo, 9
VanZant, Paige, 39

Waterson, Michelle, 57
weight classes, 5, 11–13, 17, 19–21, 26–27, 29, 35–37, 40–42, 46–47, 49–53, 57–59
White, Dana, 25, 27
World Judo Championships, 25
World Wrestling Entertainment (WWE), 32
wrestling, 18, 32, 42

Xiong, Jing Nan, 52

Zhang Weili, 5–7, 37–38, 40
Zingano, Cat, 29–30